READ ALL THESE

NATE THE GREAT

DETECTIVE STORIES

BY MARJORIE WEINMAN SHARMAT

WITH ILLUSTRATIONS BY MARC SIMONT:

Nate the Great and The CRUNCHY CHRISTMAS

by Marjorie Weinman Sharmat
and Craig Sharmat

illustrations by Marc Simont

Published by
Delacorte Press
Bantam Doubleday Dell Publishing Group, Inc.
1540 Broadway
New York, New York 10036

Library of Congress Cataloging-in-Publication Data

Sharmat, Marjorie Weinman.
Nate the Great and the crunchy Christmas / by Marjorie Weinman Sharmat
and Craig Sharmat ; illustrated by Marc Simont.
        p.   cm.
Summary: Even a deep snow the week before Christmas can't keep Nate the
Great and his dog, Sludge, from finding the special card sent to Annie's dog,
Fang, by his mother.
        ISBN 0-385-32117-1 (hc. : alk. paper)
[1. Mystery and detective stories.   2. Dogs—Fiction.   3. Christmas—Fiction.]
I. Sharmat, Craig.   II. Simont, Marc, ill.   III. Title.
PZ7.S5299Natg   1996
[Fic]—dc20   95-43575
                                                                                   CIP
                                                                                    AC

The text of this book is set in 18-point Goudy Old Style.
Book design by Julie E. Baker

Manufactured in the United States of America
October 1996
10   9   8   7   6   5   4   3   2

To my grandparents,
Nathan and Anna,
Leon and Lucille
—C.S.

I, Nate the Great,
am a detective.
I do important things.
Today I was doing something important.
I was shoveling snow.
My dog, Sludge, was chasing snowflakes.
Suddenly I heard a jingling sound.

Annie was coming up our walk
with her dog, Fang.
Fang had bells on his collar
and an elf hat on his head.
"Doesn't Fang look cute?" Annie said.
"Just like a giant elf."

Sludge looked at me.
I looked at Sludge.
We both knew that all
the bells and elves
and jingles and jangles
in the world
could not make Fang
look cute.
Fang looked hungry.
"Fang is not a happy elf,"
Annie said.
This was not good news.
"Every year, two weeks before
Christmas, Fang gets a
Christmas card from his mother
in the mail," Annie said.
"It is now a week
before Christmas

and Fang has not received
his card."
"Perhaps she didn't send it,"
I said.
"Would a mother forget Fang?"
Annie said.
I, Nate the Great,
wished I could.
"I need your help
to find the card,"
Annie said.
"I have to shovel snow,"
I said.
Fang sat down and glared at me.
I, Nate the Great,
was thinking.
It was the holiday season.

It was not a good idea
for a giant elf
to be unhappy.
"I will take your case,"
I said. "Wait here."
I went into my house.
I wrote a note to my mother.

5

Dear Mother,
I stopped shoveling snow.
I am *on* a case for
a giant elf. The snow won't go
away. Neither will
the elf. I will be back.
Love
Nate the Great

I went outside.
I spoke to Annie.
"The mailman leaves your mail
in your mailbox, right?"
"Most of the time," Annie said.
"Sometimes he drops it
on the ground
near the mailbox."

"Why does he do that?"
"Sometimes Fang is
so happy to see
the mailman that he
runs out of the house
to greet him.
The mailman drops the mail
and flees."
I, Nate the Great, knew
exactly how the mailman felt.
I said, "Then what?"
"Fang runs after the mailman.
They both disappear.
I run out to get the mail."
"So, there is no chance
for anybody else
to take that mail?"

"No chance," Annie said.
"We must go to your mailbox
and look for clues," I said.
Annie, Fang, Sludge, and I
walked through the snow.
It was crunchy under our feet.
"Are you missing any other mail?"
I asked.
"No," Annie said.

I walked up to Annie's mailbox.
It was so stuffed
that pieces of mail
were sticking out.
"I guess that today's mail
came while I was at your house,"
Annie said.
I started to open the mailbox.
"Watch out!" Annie yelled.

It was too late.
What must have been
the largest single-day collection
of holiday catalogs
ever mailed to one address
landed on me.
This was not going to be
an easy case.
"How long have you
been getting these catalogs?"
I asked.
"For about eight weeks.
I collect them," Annie said.
"I haven't had a chance
to read most of them yet.
Last year I counted
one billion nine hundred

and ninety-nine things
that you could buy."
I, Nate the Great,
did not want to know
what any of them were.
But the catalogs could be
a clue.

"I need to see the catalogs
that came last week," I said.
"About the time that Fang's card
should have arrived."
"My catalogs are all mixed up,"
Annie said. "They are in my room."
Annie, Fang, Sludge, and I
went to Annie's room.
One whole side of it was
covered with catalogs.
This was going to be
a long day.
I walked over and picked up
a catalog.

I started to look
through the pages.
An envelope fell out.
I picked it up.

"This looks like your
heating bill," I said.
"Didn't you miss getting it?"
Annie shrugged.
"It's never addressed
to me or Fang. So it
doesn't count."
I flipped through
more pages.
A postcard fell out.
It was addressed to Fang.
But I, Nate the Great,
did not think that
Fang would want to see it.
It was a reminder
from the vet
for Fang to come in
for his shots.

I picked up another catalog.
I found three envelopes in
that one.
I spoke to Annie.
"I have solved your case."
"Oh, great," Annie said.
"So where is Fang's card?"
"Solving is one thing.

Finding is another,"
I said. "The card
must be somewhere in your
catalogs. A lot of your mail
got stuck inside them.
I hope that we won't
have to look through
one billion nine hundred
and ninety-nine things
before we find the card."
Annie and I looked
through one catalog

after another.
Sludge sniffed each one.
Some of the catalogs
were for dogs.
Christmas food for dogs.
Christmas toys for dogs.
Christmas clothes for dogs.
Fang must be on a mailing list.

Envelopes kept dropping out.
But none were from Mrs. Fang.
At last I said,
"I have not solved this case.
I need clues.
Do you still have the old cards
Fang got from his mother?"
"Oh yes, Fang saves them,"
Annie said. "Here are the ones
from the last three years."
I looked at the cards.
The one from the first year
was tiny. It said
"Merry Christmas from Mother Fang.
May you eat lots of doggie bones
and grow."
The card must have worked.

The card from the second year
was bigger.
It said "Merry Christmas
from Mother Fang.
Are you eating your bones, son?
A bone a day
keeps the vet away."

The third card was even bigger.
It said "Merry Christmas from
Mother Fang.
Wear your booties in the snow.
Don't go out when it's ten below.
Eat those bones and grow, grow, grow!"
"Mrs. Fang is such a bossy mother!"
Annie said. "She knows Fang
loves bones anyway."

"Let me get this straight,"
I said. "Fang is happy
to get these cards?"
"Oh yes," Annie said.
"On Christmas Day
he jumps up on my lap.
I read him the card.
He listens to every word."
"He jumps on your *lap*?" I said.
"And he snuggles," Annie said.
"Maybe that's a clue?"
"Maybe that's a miracle,"
I said.
I, Nate the Great, was thinking.
The cards got bigger each year.
So this year's card
must be the biggest yet.
It should be easy to find.

"Who else was here last week
when the mail came?" I asked.
"Rosamond and her four cats,"
Annie said. "She was looking
for a cat catalog."
"Did you get one?"
"Yes, and I gave it to her."
"Aha! So Rosamond has
one of your catalogs.
I must go to her house."
Sludge and I left.
We crunched our way
to Rosamond's house.
On her front door
there was a big card
with a poem
and a picture of a cat
with a red cap

Santa Claws,
My cats do too.
A scritchy-scratchy
(Christmas) to you

and a white beard.
I could tell that
Rosamond was going to have
a very strange Christmas.
I knocked on the door.
Rosamond answered it.
"You are just in time
to help me decorate
my cat tree," she said.

Sludge and I walked inside.
The tree was in the
middle of the living room.
There were tuna fish cans
painted red and green
hanging from it.
All of Rosamond's cats
were sitting in the tree.
On the bottom branch was
Super Hex.
On the next branch was Big Hex.
On the next branch was Plain Hex.
On the top branch was Little Hex.
He had a ribbon around his neck
with a star hanging from it.
Rosamond smiled.
"Little Hex is the star
of my tree."

"A fine choice," I said.
"I have come to see
your cat catalog."
"Here it is,"
Rosamond said.

CAT
CATALOG
999
THINGS
TO
GIVE
YOUR CAT
for CHRISTMAS

I flipped through the pages.
"What are you looking for?"
Rosamond asked.
"A big Christmas card
from Fang's mother to Fang.
But it is not in here."
"That's dog stuff," Rosamond
said. "You won't find it in
a CATalog." Rosamond laughed.
Then she said, "I did find something.
I think it's a telephone bill."
"I will give it to Annie,"
I said. "Pretty soon she will
have no heat and no phone service.
Only catalogs."
Sludge and I walked toward the door.
"Wait, my tree isn't finished,"
Rosamond said.

"It looks finished to me," I said.
"I wish you and your cats
a Merry Christmas."
Sludge and I headed for home.
I had to think about the case.
Pancakes help me think.
At home I made potato pancakes.
I eat them every Chanukah.
"Happy Chanukah, Sludge," I said.
I gave Sludge his card
and a bone.
Sludge wagged his tail,
sniffed the card,
and started to eat the bone.

Crunch! Munch! Crunch!
"You are having a crunchy
Chanukah," I said. "Do
you know what *I* want
for the holiday?"
Sludge looked up.
"Clues!" I said.
I was thinking,
Do I have *any?*

I knew a lot of facts.
But were they *clues*?
I knew that Fang's card
was big.
I knew that when Fang
greeted the mailman
he dropped the mail
and ran for his life.
I knew that Annie had a strong lap.
Forget that one.
I knew that Rosamond had
the world's strangest
Christmas tree.
Forget that one too.
I knew that Mrs. Fang
was a bossy mother.
She kept after Fang
to eat bones.

But dogs love bones anyway.
I looked at Sludge.
He kept making crunching sounds
with his bone.
Hmm.
Was he trying to tell me something?
He was.
He knew what I had to do
to solve this case.
He knew that I, Nate the Great,
had to think like a dog!
I did not want to do that.
But I had to find the card.
"Come," I said to Sludge.
Sludge and I rushed back
to Annie's house.
It was hard to do.

The snow was getting
deeper and deeper.
I handed the telephone bill
to Annie. Then I said,
"There is a clue in
Fang's old Christmas cards.
Each year the cards
got bigger.
But that's not the clue.
Each year Mrs. Fang
got bossier.

She sent stronger messages
for Fang to eat bones.
That's a clue."
"So where is this year's
message?" Annie asked.
"I, Nate the Great, say
that Fang has it."
"Fang?"
"Yes. He found the envelope
on the ground
next to the mailbox."
Annie looked at Fang.
"I knew you were
a very smart dog," she said.
"But I didn't know that
you knew how to read."

"He doesn't," I said.
"But he knows how to sniff
and to hide things.
Tell me, does he have
a favorite hiding place?"
"Yes. Somewhere in
the backyard," Annie said.
"Follow me," I said.
Annie, Fang, and Sludge
followed me to the backyard.

It was covered with snow.
There was no trail.
"Look for a hump
or bump
in the snow," I said.
"It might be covering a hump
or bump of dirt
where Fang dug."
"I see one over there," Annie said.
"We must dig there," I said.
Annie and I started to dig.
Fang and Sludge watched.
"Why are *we* digging?" Annie asked.
"Isn't that what *dogs* do?"
I stared at Annie.
"Dig," I said.
Annie and I dug up a ball.

A shoe.

And a big, thick, soggy envelope.

"Hey, it has Fang's name on it!"

Annie said.

She handed it to Fang.

Fang tore open the envelope.

There was a bone inside.

With a card tied to it.
It said "Merry Christmas from
Mother Fang. *Eat!*"
"I, Nate the Great,
say that every year
Mrs. Fang told
Fang to eat bones.
Her message got stronger.
At last she sent Fang . . .
a real bone!

It must have come on a day
when Fang greeted the mailman.
The mail fell to the ground.
Fang sniffed the envelope.
He knew what was inside.
He ran off with it
and buried it in the dirt.
Then the snow covered it.
We uncovered it.
Now Fang will have
a crunchy Christmas.
Case solved."
Annie looked at Fang.
"You naughty elf.
You made us look
for the card
and you were hiding it
all this time."

Annie looked at me.
"Maybe this is what
elves do at Christmas time."
"No," I said. "This is
what dogs do all the time."
"How did you figure
that out?" Annie asked.
"I, Nate the Great, had to
think like a . . . detective,"
I said.
I turned to leave.
This was the last time
I would take a case
for a gigantic elf.
An elf who did not need me
in the first place.
An elf who already knew

what it took me
three and one half hours
to find out.
Suddenly the elf
dropped his bone.
Maybe he knew that
Christmas was not
until next week.
He rushed up to me.
He started to lick me.

He jingled while he licked.
"He's saying 'Happy Holidays,' "
Annie said.
"He's saying '*I'm hungry*,' " I said.
"Give this hardworking elf
an extra bone
so he can save his mother's
for Christmas."
Sludge and I started to walk away.
"Fang will love you forever," Annie said.

Sludge and I walked faster.

We headed home.

Snow was still falling.

Three and one half hours of it.

To shovel.

Maybe it would melt if I waited.

A month.

Sludge and I went up our walk.

Candles were shining in the window.

It was time for one more card . . .